HODDER'S YEAR OF STORIES
for the NATIONAL YEAR OF READING

A special introduction by Pippa Goodhart
for *Hodder's December Story Book*

The first books that I enjoyed were read aloud to my brother
and sister and me each bedtime. I was lucky to be read to
because I was very slow at learning to read. When I finally
learned to read to myself I discovered how stories can take
you into all kinds of experiences. I read more and more. The
best stories are exciting ones that make me believe they're
true so that I care what happens in them. I like stories that
leave me thinking about them long after I've finished reading.
Do you?
A true story.

Hodder
Children's
Books

a division of Hodder Headline plc

Other Hodder books by Pippa Goodhart

Locket Escapes
Flying Lessons

Milly

PIPPA GOODHART

ILLUSTRATED BY
JASON COCKCROFT

Hodder
Children's
Books

A division of Hodder Headline plc

Text copyright © 1997 Pippa Goodhart
Illustrations Copyright © 1997 Jason Cockcroft

First Published in Great Britain in 1997
by Hodder Children's Books

This paperback edition published in Great Britain
in 1998 by Hodder Children's Books

A Catalogue record for this book is available from the
British Library

ISBN 0 340 67274 9

Printed and bound in Great Britain by
The Guernsey Press Co. Ltd., Vale, Guernsey, Channel Islands

Hodder Children's Books
A Division of Hodder Headline plc
338 Euston Road
London NW1 3BH

*For my mother and father
and all who went before them*

CHAPTER ONE

ALICE KICKED HER BOOTS OFF AND PULLED AT
her gloves with her teeth. "Mum!" she called
as she threw down her coat. "Mum?"

"In here!" called her mother. Alice skated
her socked feet over the shiny hall floor,
through to the back room. Her mother was
lying on a pile of cushions on the floor. She
had her legs curled up and her head on her
hands.

"You look like Catkin!" said Alice. Catkin

7

was Grandad's kitten. "It's freezing outside!" Alice's mother held out an arm to welcome Alice into the warmth from the fire. Then she took Alice's hands in her own and blew warm breath on them.

"You've got twigs in your hair," she said.

Alice pulled bits out. "Dad's just coming. There were loads of people helping at the bonfire and it's huge! Grandad says it's probably the biggest bonfire the village has ever had. He thinks it'll get so hot that it'll crack the cobbles!"

Alice's mother smiled and yawned.

"Aren't you excited?" asked Alice. "I am! Come on, I want to dance!"

Alice took hold of her mother's hands and heaved her up off the floor. Then they swung round together in a dizzy dance until they were laughing and panting too much to go on.

"When I think about the bonfire and the fireworks I feel funny inside!" said Alice.

Her mother leaned against a table and stroked a hand over her bulging tummy. "I feel funny too," she panted. "But I don't think it's got anything to do with fireworks. I think that it's because this baby is ready to be born!"

"Now?" Alice put a hand onto her mother's stomach. It felt warm and hard. There was a person inside there. "Will the baby be born tonight? How long will it take? What are we going to call it?"

Mum put an arm around Alice. "It could take quite a time. It might not be born before tomorrow."

"But," said Alice, "it's New Year's Eve tonight so that means the baby might not be born before next year!"

Her mother laughed. "That's true! What a night to be born!"

Then Alice suddenly thought of something. "What about the party?" she asked. "What about the bonfire and fireworks? What about me while you're having the baby?"

"It's all planned," said her mother. "Grandad will look after you. He's got something very special to do tonight, and you can help him with it."

"More special than the bonfire and fireworks?" asked Alice.

"Wait and see!" said her mother.

Alice heard the back door bang. "Dad!" she shouted as she ran to him. "Dad, the baby is going to be born tonight!"

Dad looked over Alice's shoulder to where her mother was. He lifted his eyebrows and grinned. Alice still had urgent things to tell him. She pulled at his arm. "Listen, Dad! I want to see the bonfire and fireworks in the village. It's going to be a really good party with everybody there, but Mum says I might have to do something else with Grandad! Couldn't the baby be born a different night, then we wouldn't miss the party?"

But her father shook his head. "The big things in life happen when they are ready to happen, Alice. If the baby is ready to be born now, then now is when it should be born. And, anyway," Alice's father ruffled her hair and laughed, "I think that the arrival of your new brother or sister is more exciting than any party! And I know that what Grandad has planned can only happen tonight. Don't you worry. You're going to have a very special time!"

"But what is the thing I have to do with Grandad?" asked Alice.

"Ask him yourself," said Dad, and he nodded to the window where Grandad's hat was going past.

Grandad knocked at the door the way he always did. It went, slow, fast fast, slow, slow. Alice ran to the door and did two loud reply knocks back. Then she reached to twist the door knob and let Grandad in.

"Hello, Titch!" he said.

"I'm not a titch!"

"Well in that case, the baby can be my new little Titch, but what can I call you?"

"Grandad, what are we going to do tonight? I really really want to see the fireworks and the bonfire but the baby's spoilt that!"

"Well, you will see the fireworks!" said Grandad. "You will see them from high up in the church tower!"

"The church tower!" said Alice. "Why?"

"Because we are going to ring in the new year and the new millennium on the church bells."

"In the middle of the night?" asked Alice. She thought of the dark middle of the night when time would change and it made her feel excited–scared.

"Yes," said Grandad. He gave Alice's pony tail a gentle tug. "And before that you and I are going to make ourselves a new year's feast!"

"Can I give Catkin a feast too?"

"You can," said Grandad.

So Alice put her coat and boots back on, hugged her parents goodbye and went with Grandad out into the cold.

CHAPTER TWO

THE STREET LIGHTS WERE JUST COMING ON AS
Alice and Grandad walked down the road to
Grandad's house. There was noise and chatter
from the people getting the party ready in
front of the pub. The bonfire was a tall dark
mountain of sticks and planks that reached as
high as the pub sign. Tables and chairs had
been put out on the Green and two men were
hammering catherine wheels onto poles and
planting bottles into the earth ready for rockets.

Bunting and balloons flapped from trees and lamp posts. Grandad called across to the men, and they laughed back. It was all dreamy-strange. Alice looked around. Everything was silvery-grey as the last of the sunlight mixed with the orange street lights.

"Grandad?" said Alice. "Is it still day, or is it night time now?"

"It's dusk," said Grandad. "Dusk is the in between time when day is ending and night is beginning."

"Is it magical?" asked Alice.

Grandad thought for a moment before he answered. "Yes, I think it probably is," he said. "In between times are when things change, and anything is possible when there is change in the air." Then Grandad squeezed Alice's hand tight. "And tonight is full of changes. Tonight sees the end of a day, the end of a month, and the end of a year. That's the same as any new year. But this one is also the end of a decade . . ."

Milly

"What's one of those?" asked Alice.

"A decade is ten years," answered Grandad. "And it's the end of a century. That's a hundred years. And it's the end of a millennium! A millennium is a thousand years, Alice! Just think of it! And it's a beginning at the same time as being an ending.

"Tonight is the beginning of a new day, a new month, a new year, a new decade, a new century and a new millennium! There hasn't been a new millennium for a thousand years, but tonight it happens!"

"Then it must be magic," said Alice. "Let's do wishes."

"That's a good idea," said Grandad. So they stood still on the pavement outside Grandad's house and held hands. Alice knew that you must never wish out loud if you want your wish to come true. She kept her eyes open and looked up into the grey-blue darkening sky. She frowned and thought her wish as hard as she could. Grandad closed his eyes as he wished. He was looking back at memories, and he wished more gently. Alice saw the moon in the sky. It shone pale and round.

"What are we going to have for our feast?" asked Alice.

"What would you like?"

"If I could choose anything?"

"Anything at all," said Grandad, "so long as I've got the things to make it with."

"Could we have pancakes?" asked Alice. "You make the best pancakes in the world!"

"If that's what you think, then we had better have pancakes!" said Grandad. "You can help me."

Catkin, grey and frisky, jumped out at them from behind a bush and made Alice jump.

"She thinks that she's a tiger!" said Grandad. "She still has to learn that she's just a little cat."

19

Alice picked up Catkin and held the kitten's softness to her cheek as they went into Grandad's house. "It's all right," she whispered into Catkin's ear. "I like tigers."

CHAPTER THREE

"SIFT THE FLOUR WELL," SAID GRANDAD. "WE don't want lumpy pancakes!"

Alice held the sieve over a bowl with one hand and spooned flour into it with the other. Her nose itched, but there were no hands left to scratch her nose with so she just wrinkled it and tried to ignore the tickle. Catkin tried to catch the handle of the spoon as Alice stirred. Some of the flour flicked onto Catkin's grey fur. It made her look like a ghostly old cat.

Alice laughed.

"You concentrate!" said Grandad. He handed her a wire whisk and slowly began to pour a mixture of egg and milk in a river down the side of Alice's flour mountain. "Now whisk away! These have got to be the finest pancakes ever!"

Alice held the bowl still and whisked until her arm ached while Grandad poured. Gradually the dry flour and the wet eggy milk came together to make a thick sloppy batter.

"Do you know something, Alice?" asked Grandad. "Did you know that you can give a hundred people the same flour, eggs and milk and yet the pancakes they make with those ingredients would all turn out quite differently?"

"How do you mean?" Alice itched her nose with the back of her hand.

"Well," said Grandad. "Some folks would make their pancakes thick, some thin, some crisp, some soggy. Smooth or lumpy, big or small, they'd all be different. People are like pancakes."

Alice laughed.

"It's true!" said Grandad. "Children can grow up with the same parents, in the same home and with the same chances, and yet they will all turn out quite different! There's another way that pancakes are like children too. They both need plenty of rest! We'll leave this mixture to rest in the bowl while we lay the table for our feast."

"And feed Catkin," said Alice. She wiped her hands on a cloth and itched her nose properly at last.

"And feed Catkin," said Grandad.

Grandad opened the tin of cat food. He let Alice plop it out of the tin into Catkin's bowl. Catkin quivered with purrs as she rubbed herself against Alice's legs. As Alice crouched down to put the bowl on the floor, Catkin jumped lightly onto her lap.

"Careful!" said Alice, lifting the bowl up high. Catkin pushed her head into Alice's

jumper, her eyes half closed and her claws
working in and out.

"Ow, that hurt!"

Alice pushed Catkin down onto the floor
and quickly put the bowl of food beside her.
In and out went Catkin's little pink tongue, lap
lap lap. Alice stroked down the kitten's soft
back.

"Do you think that she likes us?" she asked. "Or does she just like the food?"

"Oh, she likes us all right," said Grandad. "But when she's hungry, food is far more important than people. Do you agree with her?"

Alice thought about that. "No," she said. "I like food, but people are more important."

"That shows you're growing up," said Grandad. "You'll find that your new baby will agree with Catkin!"

Grandad took a tablecloth out of a drawer. "Now help me with this, will you? I think we should make things posh for our feast."

Alice and Grandad found the four corners of the tablecloth, and they lifted the cloth up and then down and tugged it smooth over the table.

"Candles," said Grandad. He took two brass candle sticks down from a shelf. He whittled bits off the bottom of two waxy white

new candles to make them fit the holders.
Then he winked at Alice and said, "Don't tell
your mother!" and he let her light the candles
by herself. She put them very carefully into
the middle of the table.

Grandad turned the electric light off and
the flickering candle light made the flowers on
the tablecloth look as if they were moving and
alive. Alice fingered the knobbly stitching as
Grandad put out plates and spoons and forks.

"Those flowers are called forget-me-nots,"
said Grandad. "My mother - your great grand-
mother - sewed those flowers, oh, almost sixty
years ago. Your Great Aunt Jean and I must
have been round about your age when she
made it. I remember because it was when
Mother broke her leg. She couldn't walk for
several weeks and she sat with her leg propped
up and stitched at all those flowers while Jean
and I tried to do the housework." Grandad
chuckled. "I don't think we were very good at

it! I remember breaking one of Mother's favourite jugs and hiding it at the back of a shelf."

Grandad stopped laying the table. "I wonder if she ever found it? She never said anything about it to me. Anyway, I enjoyed that time in spite of the housework because it meant that my mother had lots of time to talk to me. I remember sitting with her and watching her fast fingers working away while we talked about me and what I wanted to do when I grew up."

"What did you want to be?" asked Alice.

"Oh, the usual thing in those days," said Grandad. "I wanted to be an engine driver on the trains. I wanted that more than anything." Then Grandad looked across at Alice in the candlelight. "Would you like to have this cloth?" he asked.

"Do you mean to keep?" asked Alice.

"To keep and to use and to remember your great granny by," said Grandad.

"I'd like that," said Alice. Great Granny sounded nice. "When it's old enough, I'll tell our baby about you talking to your mum while she made it."

"You do that," said Grandad.

CHAPTER FOUR

"WHAT SORT OF PANCAKES DO YOU FANCY FOR the first course of our feast?" asked Grandad. "Do you like cheese? I've got some nice orange cheese. Or apple? I've got apples from my garden."

Alice couldn't decide. "Could we have both at once?" she asked, so Grandad made a pancake for each of them with grated cheese and slices of apple rolled up inside.

"Yum," said Alice.

"Shall we give these pancakes a name?" said Grandad. "Shall we call them Millennium Pancakes, and then we can remember them by name for another time?"

Grandad did the pancakes differently for pudding. He tossed them flip-flap over in the air and landed them back down into the pan to crisp. Alice and Catkin watched as Grandad tossed each pancake, waiting for him to drop one on the floor, but he never missed the pan. And when each pancake was crisped on both sides, he slid it out of the pan, flat onto a warm plate.

Grandad had a squeeze of lemon juice and a sprinkle of sugar on his. Alice dribbled honey from very high up onto hers. Grandad didn't tell her off, even when a bit spilt on Great Granny's table cloth.

"Bet I can do it from even higher!" he said, and he did, without spilling any! He was an expert.

Alice wondered whether Grandad practised dribbling honey from high up when he was on his own in his house. When you were old you could do things like that, and nobody told you off. Being a baby was a bit like that too. You could be very messy and nobody minded. Alice wondered about her baby brother or sister.

"Will the baby be like me?" she asked Grandad.

"I expect that it will be like you in some ways," he said. "But I'm sure that it will be different in others. Jean and I aren't much like each other, and we are brother and sister."

Alice thought about Grandad being a little boy. "Have you got any photographs of when you were little?" she asked.

"One or two," said Grandad. "Would you like to see them?"

So, once Alice had helped wash up and Grandad had put things away, Grandad got out his photographs. Alice snuggled next to him on the sofa so that she could see the photographs as Grandad turned the pages of his scrap book. Most of the photos were in black and white. They were pictures of lots of old-fashioned people that Alice didn't recognise. There was a man in a soldier's uniform who was standing stiffly and staring at the camera. There were a group having a picnic at the seaside. There was a little boy on his own at the seaside. He was grinning and holding up a jelly fish for the person with the camera to see. Alice recognised him.

"That's you, Grandad!"

Even though the little boy had lots of sticking up hair and Grandad was a bit bald. Even though the little boy was wearing baggy shorts and Grandad always wore trousers. Even though the boy was young and Grandad was old, you could see  that they were the same person because the eyes and the grin were the same. Alice looked and knew that she would have liked to play with the boy Grandad.

"Can I see more?" asked Alice.

There was a picture of Great Aunt Jean in a frilly dress that Grandad called a frock.

"Is it nice having a sister?" asked Alice.

"Most of the time it is," said Grandad.

And there was a smiling lady with a funny hat on that covered one of her eyes.

"That's my mother," Grandad told her. "She was the one who made the forget-me-not tablecloth." At the bottom of the photograph somebody had written, 'Alice Brotherton.'

"Was she called Alice too?" asked Alice.

"Yes," said Grandad. "Didn't you know? You were named after your great granny. You're a bit like her in some ways. You've got the same sideways smile that she had!"

Alice liked hearing that.

There were aunts and uncles, grandparents and even great grandparents in Grandad's photographs. The further back you went, the more grandparents there were.

"You have two parents," said Grandad. "Your mother and your father. Each of them have a mother and father of their own and so that gives you four grandparents. Those grandparents have parents too and that means you have eight great grandparents, and it goes on doubling in number each time you go back a generation."

"So how many great great great, however many times great, grandparents did I have a thousand years ago?" asked Alice.

Grandad laughed. "Well, now. That takes a bit of working out!" He got up and found a pencil and paper and his calculator. "Now supposing that a new generation of babies was born every twenty-five years," he said. "That would mean forty generations in a thousand years." Grandad poked at his calculator and made surprised muttering sounds as he wrote down numbers that got longer and longer.

Catkin was curled up fast asleep on Alice's

lap. Catkin wasn't interested in the past. Alice herself was beginning to feel sleepy when Grandad at last pushed back his chair. "Done it" he said. "I've worked it out. Look at this, Alice!" and he showed her a number. It said 549755813888. "That's five hundred and forty-nine billion, seven hundred and fifty-five million, eight hundred and thirteen thousand, eight hundred and eighty-eight! That's how many grandparents you had a thousand years ago!"

Alice couldn't begin to think of that number of people. Trying to imagine eighty-eight was bad enough. Hundreds of billions was impossible.

Grandad was scratching his head. "It's hard to believe, but whatever way you look at it, an awful lot of people have played a part in making you, *you*, my Alice! You are a mixture of each one of them! And the new baby has been made from exactly the same recipe of billions of people!"

"But the baby will be like a pancake and come out different!"

"That's right!" said Grandad.

"Do you think the baby might be born yet?" asked Alice.

CHAPTER FIVE

GRANDAD RANG ALICE'S HOUSE, BUT THE BABY still hadn't been born.

"We'll have to be patient," said Grandad. He looked at his watch. "Nine o'clock. I think that the best thing for you and me to do is have a rest before it's time to go up to the church."

"But what about the bonfire and fireworks?" asked Alice. She was feeling droopy-tired. It was past her usual bedtime but she didn't want to miss any of the special things.

"Don't worry," said Grandad. "You won't miss them, I promise. The bonfire will go on all night and the fireworks won't start until midnight. You don't want to be too tired to enjoy them when it is midnight, do you?"

Grandad got a blanket and tucked Alice up on the sofa.

Alice lay, snug on a cushion that smelt of Grandad with Catkin snuggled beside her. Alice closed her eyes. She thought about all those people who were a part of her. They had been born and grown up and had babies and died a thousand years ago. They had been real people, just like her and Grandad and Mum and Dad and the baby. Alice opened her eyes again.

"What were all those people like, Grandad?"

"Well now," said Grandad as he settled himself into his big chair. "They were people with just the same sorts of feelings and needs as you or me, but they lived in a different way in those days. I suppose that there just could have been a king and queen amongst them, but I doubt it! Most of them would have been farmers because in those days most people spent their time growing their own food. Some might have had a trade. They might have been blacksmiths or leather workers or wood-workers. Some of them were probably Viking people from over the sea, coming to settle and make new homes in Britain."

Catkin yawned a pink mouth full of teeth. It made Alice yawn too.

Grandad went on, "The Viking people won't have spoken the same language as the people who already lived here. They might have stolen things from them. I'm afraid that some of your grandparents probably didn't like each other at all, Alice. They probably fought each other and maybe even killed each other all those years ago!"

"But do you think that they would have killed each other if they'd known?" asked Alice.

"Known what?" asked Grandad.

"Known that they would all join together in the end to make me!" said Alice.

"Perhaps if they had thought of that they might have been better friends. It would be nice to think so, anyway," said Grandad. "Now, close your eyes and go to sleep."

CHAPTER SIX

ALICE SLEPT. AS GRANDAD'S CLOCK AND HIS
snores marked the time away, Alice dreamed of
children who might wonder about her at the
next millennium in a thousand years' time. She
would be their thirty-eight times great grand-
mother! They might be living on the moon by
then. They might be able to travel back in
time and visit her!

Time tick-tocked on. Then Grandad was
gently shaking her shoulder.

"Wake up, Chick! It's time we were off to church to see to those bells."

Alice yawned and stretched.

"No news of the baby yet," said Grandad. He handed her a mug of cocoa. "This will help you wake up."

Alice sat up.

She could hear the muffled sound of voices and music from outside. They were daytime sounds, but the dark at the window showed that it was night-time. Alice hoped that it wouldn't be too dark outside.

Grandad shut Catkin into the kitchen.

"She might get frightened when the fireworks start," he said.

"And she might get lost in the dark," said Alice.

But Grandad said, "No. Cats can find their way even when there is no light at all. They can feel their way, using their whiskers."

"Can you feel the way with your whiskers

too?" asked Alice, and she tugged at Grandad's beard.

"No!" laughed Grandad. "All my whiskers do is keep my chin warm!"

Alice and Grandad put on coats and gloves and opened the door into the night. Outside the noises were louder. There were cooking smells, and coloured lines of fairy lights bobbed in the wind. The bonfire was alive with crackling orange fire and its heat made Alice wince as she walked past. There were lots of people that Alice knew. She waved to some of her friends from school who were playing hide and seek in and out of the dark shadows.

Alice lifted Grandad's gloved hand and gave it a kiss.

"What was that for?" asked Grandad.

"Because I'm glad that I'm with you," said Alice.

"Well, so am I!" said Grandad, and he squeezed her hand tight.

Milly

The big church door creaked as Grandad opened it, and inside the church was musty and echoey-dark like a cave. The nativity scene surrounded by holly and ivy and Christmas roses was lit and it glowed in the darkness.

Alice looked at Mary made of clay as she bent over the crib with newborn baby Jesus in it. It was two thousand years since Jesus was born, but people still remembered it.

Grandad clicked switches to light the stairway up the tower.

"Up we go," he said.

The steps were made of cold hard stone, shaped like slices of cake. They wound round and up and Alice watched her feet and made sure that she stepped onto the widest part of each step. The steps went on and on and Alice began to feel dizzy, but at last they came to an end in the corner of an empty room.

"Here we are," said Grandad.

Alice looked. There were windows on

three sides of the room. They had big sills that you could sit on. There was an old bit of carpet in the middle of the floor and there was a cupboard on one side. But the only other things in the room were long, looped ropes that hung down from holes in the ceiling. It wasn't what Alice had expected.

"Where are the bells?" she asked.

"The bells are higher up," said Grandad. "Goodness me, if we had them ringing in the room with us, we'd be deaf in no time!"

"But can I see them?"

"Yes," said Grandad. "We can climb up to the bells if you like. But you must be extra careful, because it's ladders all the way."

The ladders were scary. They bounced with every step. There was a cold breeze coming from windows that had no glass in them, and the only light came from Grandad's big torch. A bird flapped near Alice. The top of the tower was a strange half-inside, half-outside place.

Alice was glad that Grandad was close behind
and with his arms on either side of her as she
climbed. At the top of the last ladder Alice
dared to look up. And there were the bells.

 They hung from great wooden spoked wheels mounted on a criss-cross of beams. Alice touched the nearest bell. It was hard and very cold. It must be very heavy, she thought. The bells looked strong and powerful, hanging in the shadows, waiting to make their great sounds. Alice had the feeling that they had been around for a long time, perhaps even before Great Granny Alice was born. "How old are they?" she whispered.

"Some of them are very old indeed," said Grandad. "Look at this one over here." Grandad shone his torch on the smallest of the bells. It was darker than the others. He stroked a hand over its curved surface. "See this?" he said, and he pointed to some lumpy writing around the top of the bell. "It's in a language called Latin. In the very old days, any writing that was done was done in Latin.

"Why?" asked Alice.

"I don't really know why," said Grandad. "But this bit of Latin says 'Semper Eadem' and then there is the date, 1458. That was the year that this bell was made, so it's over five hundred years old! Semper Eadem means 'always the same'. I suppose they wrote that because it is true of bells. They are always the same. This old bell will have been rung in war and peace, for deaths and for births and it rings the same note for every occasion, always the same through all those hundreds of years."

"Do they ring the same now as they did hundreds of years ago?" asked Alice.

"Well," said Grandad. "What people do with bells changes, but the bells themselves don't. Nowadays the bells are mostly rung for church services or by bell-ringers wanting to practice or ring peals."

"What's a peal?" asked Alice.

"A peal is when you ring the bells over and

over again in a different order every time."

"That's not always the same, then, is it?" said Alice.

"No, you're right about that!" agreed Grandad. "But each bell sounds its one note, always the same. It is what is done with that sound that is different. These bells rang when your mother and father were married. Perhaps you remember them ringing when your Granny Milly had died." Granny Milly had been Grandad's wife. He was quiet for a moment before going on. "In the old days the bells were used for more than that. In the days before people had watches or clocks a bell would be rung to mark different times of day. And they were used as an alarm, too. If there was a fire in the village, or soldiers were on their way to attack, then a bell was rung to tell people to hurry and bring help."

"What was the best time the bells ever rang?" asked Alice.

"I can't tell you what was the best time in the five hundred years that the little bell has rung because I've only been around for a few of them!" said Grandad. "But I know what seemed to me to be the best time of all, and that was at the ending of the Second World War. These bells rang out and we children heard them from the village school. We all went quiet when we heard them, and then we looked at one another and we knew. We knew that the bells were telling us that the war was over! For a minute or so we all just sat, listening and smiling our heads off, and then we all went mad! We threw our school books in the air and ran outside!"

"What did the teacher say?" asked Alice.

"I think she probably joined in with us!" said Grandad. "Remember, we had lived through six years of war – more than half our lives – and our fathers had nearly all gone to be soldiers. Some of the fathers had been killed or wounded in the war, and now it was over! I knew that those bells were telling me that my dad, who I hardly knew, was safe. I knew he would be coming home soon. That was the best time those bells have rung for me. They sounded different that day." Then Grandad grinned. "But they weren't different, of course. They were 'Semper Eadem', always the same."

CHAPTER SEVEN

ALICE LOOKED AT THE WRITING AROUND THE
top of the old bell.

"That writing goes on forever too, doesn't
it?" said Alice. "You can read it on and on
round the bell forever and never get to the
end."

"That's true," said Grandad. "Circles and
rings do go on forever. That's why we have
wedding rings as a symbol of the sort of love
that goes on forever. Look!" Grandad held out

his left hand for Alice to see. On the finger next to the little finger was a rather thin and scratched ring of gold that shone back the light from Grandad's torch. "Your Granny gave me this ring when we got married," he told Alice. "Now, even though she isn't here any more, I feel that ring on my finger and I know that her love is still with me."

"Is that how space goes on forever?" asked Alice. "And time? Are they rings too?"

"Oh," said Grandad. "I don't know about those things, Chick! That question is too clever for me. Perhaps you'll grow into a famous scientist one day and discover whether or not that's true. Then you can tell me! I do know something, though. I know that in all the years that these bells have rung, they have never yet rung for a new millennium! Tonight will be the very first time that any of these bells ring in a millennium. What do you think of that?"

"And they can ring 'Hello' for the new

baby at the same time!" said Alice.

"They certainly can," said Grandad.

"Now," said Grandad. "Before we go back down, I've got a job to do." He showed Alice some rounded leather shapes with cords hanging from them. "Can you guess what these are for?" he asked.

Alice counted. There were eight of them and there were eight bells. They must be something to do with the bells, but Alice couldn't guess what. "I give up," she said.

So Grandad told her. "They're muffles. I'm going to tie one of them onto the clapper of each bell. That's this bit." Grandad lifted up the long metal rod with a rounded end that hung down inside the little bell. "This is what hits the bell and makes it sound. Watch."

Grandad swung the clapper to hit the side of the bell and a clear loud note sounded that Alice felt in her throat. "Now watch how I change that sound," he said. He tied the leather muffle to cover one side of the round clapper end. Then he swung the clapper to the side of the bell again. This time the note that sounded from the bell was the same, but it was quieter, softer. "See?" said Grandad. "It makes the bell sound loud as the clapper goes one way, and soft as as goes the other. It makes the bell sound as if it has an echo."

Alice liked the soft echo sound best.

"What's it for?" she asked.

"It's to make the bells sound sad as we ring goodbye to the old year and the old millennium. We'll ring the bells like that before midnight. Then, while the clock strikes twelve and the year and the millennium change, I'll send Peter running up the ladders to untie the muffles. Peter will do it faster than I can manage these days. Then he'll have to hurry back down and we'll ring in the new year and the new millennium with the full proud sound of unmuffled bells."

"Will you be doing the ringing?" asked Alice.

"I'll ring the old treble bell that I showed you, but only to ring goodbye to the old year," said Grandad. "I want to ring goodbye to all those years that have been good to me. But I'll leave ringing in the new time to the younger ones. The new millennium will be their time, after all. And it will be yours too, Alice. Yours and that baby's." Grandad looked seriously at Alice. "Use the time well, won't you?"

Alice nodded, and Grandad smiled again.

"Come on," he said. "Back down the ladders. Just you wait 'til you hear the bells ring in the new! We aren't usually allowed to ring for long at new years because some people don't like the noise in the middle of the night. But tonight is special! Tonight we'll wake up anyone who's asleep in bed, and I don't care! We've waited a thousand years for a new millennium, and I'm blowed if I'm going to let anyone sleep through it! " Grandad's eyes twinkled with naughtiness. "I dare say there'll be complaints to the vicar tomorrow and I shall have to apologise, but tonight the whole village is going to hear the new millennium arrive, whether they like it or not!"

Alice laughed. "Will Catkin hear it?"

"She will."

"And Mum and Dad?" asked Alice.

"They will hear it loud and clear," said Grandad. "And the midwife will too! You never know, our bells might be the first sound that the baby hears outside your mother's tummy!"

CHAPTER EIGHT

WHEN ALICE AND GRANDAD GOT BACK DOWN
the ladders, the other ringers were beginning to
arrive. Alice knew most of them. Peter worked
in the village shop, so she knew him very well.

"Hello, Alice!" he said. "I thought you
would be down at the village party!"

"I was going to be," Alice told him. "Only
the baby's being born so I'm with Grandad."

She hugged her arms around herself as

excitement fizzed through her at the thought of the baby. I do hope I like it when it grows into a proper person, she thought.

Grandad and the others began ringing up the bells. Alice quietly climbed onto one of the wide window sills and looked out from the tower. She looked down on the village. There was brightness and noise and movement around the bonfire, and sparks went up fast into the sky above it. Street lights edged the two roads of the village and some of the houses had front door lights on and Christmas trees lit in their windows. There was only one house that had lights on upstairs and downstairs. That was Alice's house. Alice smiled and rested her chin on her hands. She could see a car that she didn't recognise parked just outside her house. It probably belonged to the midwife who was helping Mum have the baby.

For a moment Alice longed to be there in the house with them all, but then Grandad was

Milly

patting her shoulder.

"We're going to start ringing out the old year," he told her. "Will you be all right, sitting on this cold window sill? Let me make it a bit more cosy for you." Grandad made a soft cushion of coats for Alice to sit on. "Now," he said. "You mustn't try to talk to any of us while we are ringing. We have to concentrate. You sit and eat this and enjoy the view."

Grandad handed Alice a bar of chocolate. "O.K., Chick?"

Alice nodded.

"You're a good girl," said Grandad.

Grandad stood in the circle with the other ringers and took hold of his rope. "Look to," he said. "Treble's going. She's gone." And one after another the ringers' arms pulled down and a beautiful mournful clang-bong song of muffled bells swayed the church tower and boomed into Alice.

Alice watched the ringers with their intent

faces and up-and-down arms for a while. Then she turned and looked out of the window again. Biting into the chocolate, she looked towards Grandad's house. It looked so tiny from up here. She imagined how very very tiny Catkin would look if she could see her. Alice wondered whether Catkin minded being all alone in the kitchen. She was glad that she wasn't on her own.

Alice looked along the road between Grandad's house and the church. Things looked bigger, the nearer they were to the church. When she looked straight down into the churchyard below she could see things quite clearly so long as they weren't in one of the shadowy corners. There was the tree and the gravestone that marked Granny Milly's grave. The soft booming bells seemed to ring for Granny Milly who was dead but whose love went on. Alice thought about her Granny. She remembered collecting fir cones with her one afternoon. They filled two buckets with fir cones and Granny put most of them next to the fire place. She said that they made a winter's fire smell sweet. But she let Alice choose some of the nicest cones and showed her how to turn them into hedgehogs. Alice still had one of the hedgehogs in her bedroom.

Suddenly, the ringing stopped. The quiet seemed loud after all the noise. It hummed in Alice's ears.

"Come on, Alice," said Grandad. "You come and join us, now. It's very nearly midnight! Hold hands, everyone!"

Peter was already on his way up the ladders.

Grandad and Mrs Pott from next door held out hands to Alice. She jumped down from her window seat and took hold of their big warm hands. As she linked the last bit of the circle of people together, the clock began its slow chime. One – Two – Three – Four – Five – Six – Seven – Eight – Nine – Ten – Eleven –

and, as the clock struck Twelve, Alice lifted her arms with the rest and cheered aloud. The whole world seemed to cheer with her. A great roaring shout of joy floated up from the village below as Peter jumped down the last steps of the ladder. He took Grandad's rope and Grandad stood back with Alice as the ringers held their ropes high and Peter called, "Look to. Treble's going. She's gone." And one after the other the ropes were pulled and down swung the bells in a great glorious clanging, jangling celebration.

At the same moment the first fireworks burst bright chrysanthemum flowers of light at the window. The bells rang faster and louder than Alice had ever heard them before. Round and round they tumbled, chasing each other, top to bottom, until they suddenly clang-banged their jangling joy all together and crashed out a noise that was every note at once, piled up and down in a great heap of

sound that made Alice cover her ears and laugh.

"That should wake the new millennium all right!" shouted Grandad.

Alice's laugh turned into a yawn.

"Time to go home?" asked Grandad.

"Yes," said Alice.

As Grandad and Alice wound down the steep tower steps, the bells had stopped crashing and were ringing out a happy, loud nonsense tune.

"They're starting the peal," said Grandad. "A peal to welcome the new millennium."

CHAPTER NINE

OUTSIDE THE CHURCH THE NIGHT WAS LOUD with bells and bright with fireworks. In the distance, Alice could see somebody walking along the road towards them. It was Dad. He waved and shouted something that Alice couldn't quite hear.

Alice wanted to run.

She pulled Grandad along by the hand, but he wouldn't go as fast as she wanted, so she let go and ran by herself to Dad who was laughing and hugging her and saying something about a baby girl.

Together, they came through the front door into the warmth and brightness of home. Dad gave Alice a little push towards the stairs and then she was running again, up to Mum and Dad's room. She peeped shyly around the bedroom door and there was Mum, sitting in bed and telling her to come in and meet someone. Alice tiptoed to the old Moses basket that had once been hers.

"Oh, Mum!" she said.

For a few moments time stood still for Alice. She didn't know that her mother was talking to her. She didn't feel her father's hand on her shoulder. She didn't hear Grandad arrive, panting, at the doorway. All she saw was the crumpled, bright-eyed, frowning little person in the Moses basket. Her sister. A whole new person who might be like Alice in some ways but would be different too. A sister who she knew she would love forever, no matter what.

Alice put her thumb and her middle finger together and gently offered her finger ring to

the baby. Tiny fingers grabbed hold and held
on tight.

"What do you think we should call her?" whispered Mum.

Alice paused and thought for only a moment before answering. "I think she should be Milly. Milly to be like Granny Milly and Milly for the new millennium. Then we'll never forget the night that she was born!"

Another Story Book from Hodder Children's Books

THE DRAGON'S CHILD

Jenny Nimmo

> *'Mother, I'm falling.' With a final squeal, the*
> *dragon's child slid from his mother's back and fell*
> *earthwards through the wind.*

Dando the dragon child, abandoned by his
mother, must now survive alone. In a place
where the dreadful Doggins lurk. Only an
orphaned slave girl offers him hope. She knows
he is a magical creature, and their special
friendship keeps them both safe, for now . . .

An enchanting fantasy from the prize-winning
author of *The Snow Spider.*

HODDER'S YEAR OF STORIES
for the NATIONAL YEAR OF READING

Why not collect all twelve Story Books in *Hodder's Year of Stories?*

January	Fog Hounds, Wind Cat, Sea Mice *Joan Aiken*	0340 75274 2	£1.99 ❐
February	The Railway Cat's Secret *Phyllis Arkle*	0340 75278 5	£1.99 ❐
March	A Dog of My Own *Alan Brown*	0340 75276 9	£1.99 ❐
April	The Dragon's Child *Jenny Nimmo*	0340 75277 7	£1.99 ❐
May	Jake *Annette Butterworth*	0340 75281 5	£1.99 ❐
June	Hamish *W. J. Corbett*	0340 75275 0	£1.99 ❐
July	The Silkie *Sandra Horn*	0340 75279 3	£1.99 ❐
August	A Gift from Winklesea *Helen Cresswell*	0340 75280 7	£1.99 ❐
September	The Fox Gate *William Mayne*	0340 75282 3	£1.99 ❐
October	Dark at the Foot of the Stairs *Eileen Moore*	0340 75283 1	£1.99 ❐
November	Secret Friends *Elizabeth Laird*	0340 75284 X	£1.99 ❐
December	Milly *Pippa Goodhart*	0340 75285 8	£1.99 ❐

ORDER FORM

Please select your Year of Reading Story Books from the previous page

---

All Hodder Children's books are available at your local bookshop or newsagent, or can be ordered direct from the publisher. Just tick the titles you want and fill in the form below. Prices and availability subject to change without notice.

Hodder Children's Books, Cash Sales Department, Bookpoint, 39 Milton Park, Abingdon, OXON, OX14 4TD, UK. If you have a credit card you may order by telephone - (01235) 831700.

Please enclose a cheque or postal order made payable to Bookpoint Ltd to the value of the cover price and allow the following for postage and packing:
UK & BFPO - £1.00 for the first book, 50p for the second book, and 30p for each additional book ordered up to a maximum charge of £3.00.
OVERSEAS & EIRE - £2.00 for the first book, £1.00 for the second book, and 50p for each additional book.

Name..

Address ....

....

....

If you would prefer to pay by credit card, please complete:
Please debit my Visa/Access/Diner's Card/American Express (delete as applicable) card no.

Signature...

Expiry Date...